I0749228

# THE TALE OF THE RUSTY NAIL

TAHIR SHAH

MAHYA SADEGHI

# THE TALE OF THE RUSTY NAIL

*A Teaching Story*

TAHIR SHAH

MAHYA SADEGHI

MMXXIV

Secretum Mundi Publishing Ltd
124 City Road
London
EC1V 2NX
United Kingdom

www.secretum-mundi.com
info@secretum-mundi.com

First published by Secretum Mundi Publishing Ltd, 2024
A version of this story originally appeared in *Scorpion Soup* by Tahir Shah, 2013

THE TALE OF THE RUSTY NAIL



Artwork drawn by Mahya Sadeghi



A CIP catalogue record for this title is available from the British Library.

ISBN 978-1-915876-07-2

VERSION 05012024

Visit the author's website:
Tahirshah.com

A donkey with two backs is still a donkey.

*Moroccan saying*

## Teaching Stories

When I was small, I was told stories from morning till night.

I was told stories about genies and witches and about great birds that could carry away elephants on their wings… and stories about distant kingdoms and magical lands ruled by warrior kings.

I was told stories of good and bad… stories of hope and others of despair.

I was even told stories about stories.

And all the while, I listened, amazed.

The more I listened, the more my mind worked… and the more I came to understand that these stories had a power about them, a secret lifeblood all of their own.

They were magical instruments, machineries that could alter states of mind and change the way we think.

But most importantly of all, stories can teach us, without us realizing that they are doing so at all.

Part of the default programming of man, stories are within us all.

Born into us, they make us who we are – they make us human.

Since earliest childhood, I have feasted on stories as a way of learning about the world, and learning about myself. They have been my dictionary and my encyclopaedia, my classroom, my guide, and my very best friend.

To descend down through the layers of stories is to be reborn, into a dominion of fantasy – one touched by real magic.

Pre-eminent within the great treasuries of tales, it is teaching stories like this one that have shown me the path to follow beyond the next horizon, and have made me the man I am.

Tahir Shah

There was once in Ethiopia a tyrannical emperor who spent his days counting the sacks of treasure in his many vaults.

They were piled from floor to ceiling in rows of a hundred and one – each of them bursting with rubies and emeralds, diamonds and gold.

Each year, as the emperor's wealth doubled once and then again through taxes and foreign wars, the people grew more eager for change.

Their sons slaughtered in battle, their precious savings confiscated to satisfy their ruler's insatiable greed, they sought a secret way by which to end his reign of tyranny.

The problem was that the emperor rarely left his palace – a vast marble structure twenty storeys high, set on the banks of the sprawling River Walaqa, a tributary of the Blue Nile.

The kingdom had been plundered
to construct the palace and to fill
its magazines with treasure.

With such poverty surrounding him, the emperor had no interest in ever leaving the luxurious quarters of his home.

So he reclined in his gardens, or in his grand salons, and allowed his retinue of servants to drop peeled grapes into his mouth, one at a time.

Every so often the secret police caught a group of citizens conspiring against their emperor.

The conspirators would be dragged away, hung, drawn, and quartered in the main square.

Then their heads were skewered
onto spikes as a warning to others.

Now, in this land there lived a small boy.
He had never known his parents because
they had been imprisoned in the Slate Tower,
which lay on an island in the middle of
the River Walaqa.

Their crime was daring to question out loud why their emperor required so many sacks of loot when beyond his palace walls there wasn’t enough food to eat.

So the boy resided with his aunt, a fresh-faced woman with a limp who was very good to him.

His name was Rintin, and he was the cleverest boy in his school. He never said much, but when he did say something others listened, because what he said tended to be very clever indeed.

One day, Rintin was on his way back from school when he saw his elderly neighbour being led in chains towards the gallows in the main square.

On that day there were so many others in line to be hanged that the neighbour was forced to crouch down and wait his turn.

Nimbly, Rintin hurried over to
the old man, greeted him, and said:
'I will save you, I promise, I will save you.'

The wizened old man smiled at seeing the boy, then held up his wrists, weighed down as they were with manacles.

‘Keep away from me, dear Rintin,’
he said softly, ‘before they take you too.’

Charging off into the back streets, the boy
stopped at the first house he could find.
A little girl was playing with her doll outside.

'Tell your parents to go to the palace gates at dusk,' he said. 'The emperor is going to make an announcement. Your parents must spread the word!'

Clutching her doll,
the little girl ran into the house.

As for Rintin, he hurried on through the streets, warning everyone he passed to gather at the palace at dusk.

Once he had reached the end of the town,
he made his way to the banks of the river.

With the palace itself so heavily guarded, the only way to observe it unnoticed was from the water.

Borrowing a canoe from a fisherman, he pushed out, then paddled his way into the middle, halfway between the palace and the Slate Tower in which his parents were imprisoned.

Turning his back on the island, Rintin looked carefully at the pleasure dome of the emperor. Scanning the walls, he took in every detail, questioning why it was as it was.

Now, the lad's cleverness derived from the fact that he observed very keenly. Almost nothing ever escaped his attention.

He knew, for example, when a storm
was approaching, for he could sense
the trembling of the leaves.

And he could tell when his aunt was unhappy because her handkerchief smelled very faintly of salt from her tears.

Rintin's gaze moved over the blocks of marble, searching for gaps, or for an unguarded window amongst the sheering white walls.

The stones were flush together, joined in a zigzag edge so that nothing could ever prise them apart.

All afternoon, the boy gazed at the palace.

As the shadows lengthened, he felt a pang of worry. After all, the townspeople would be making their way to the gates to hear the announcement.

No one would dare stay away,
for the emperor was very strict indeed
about his announcements.

An hour before dusk, Rintin paddled the canoe a little closer to the wall, which was now deep in chill shadow.

Approaching, he noticed something strange.

Where the walls disappeared at the waterline,
there was a knotted mesh of reeds.

The palace was, it seemed, constructed on a kind of giant woven raft made from bulrushes. It was incredible that such a mighty structure could sit securely as it did on a foundation so flimsy and feeble.

Scanning the zigzag lines between the blocks of stone, Rintin noticed that there was an unevenness near the waterline.

A piece of marble had been wedged into a crack where the zigzag joins were broken – a definite force was being exerted upon it.

But stranger still was the fact that a fragment of wood, no bigger than a matchbox, had been hammered into place beside the sliver of marble.

The wood was held in place with a nail
– a bent, brown, rusty nail.

Touching a finger to his chin in contemplation, Rintin made a series of calculations.

By his reckoning, the entire palace was being held up by this single nail.

How extraordinary, he thought, that the emperor's mighty seat of power hung so precariously in the balance, and all because a craftsman had cut a corner he imagined no one would ever spot.

Paddling his canoe over to the nail, Rintin knocked it up and down with his oar until it was loose. Then, taking a deep breath, he pulled it away from the wood.

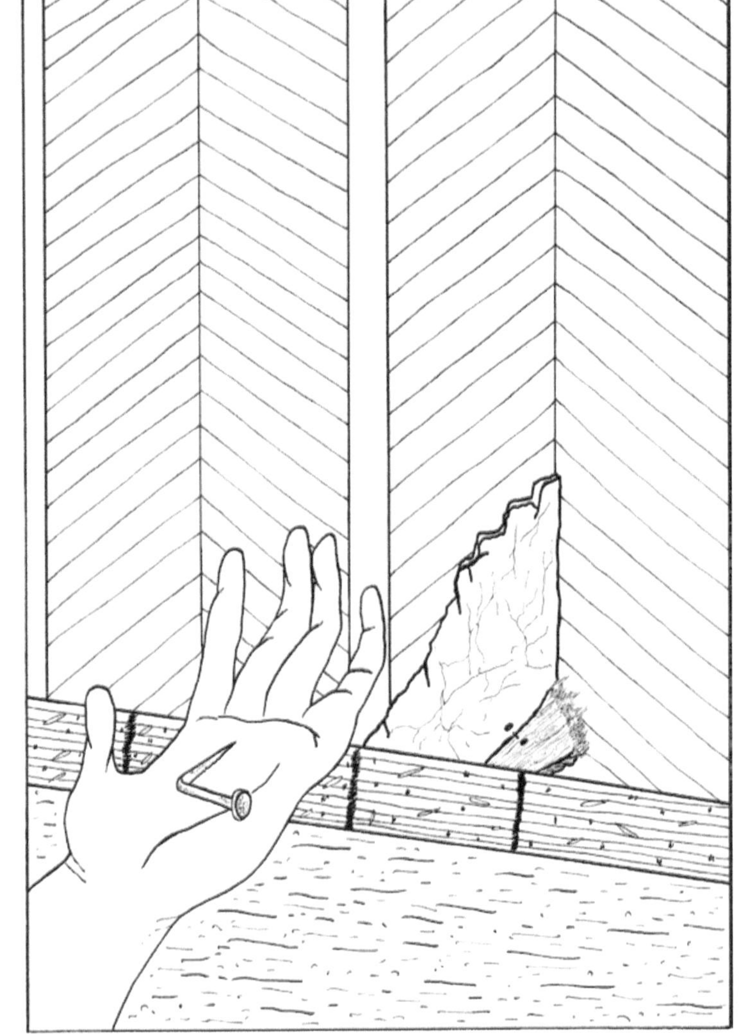

Nothing happened.

Not at first, anyway.

A minute passed.

And another.

The boy cupped a hand to his right ear and he heard something – a faintest undertone of sound.

Gasping, he grabbed the oar and paddled away as fast as he could.

A moment later, there was a deafening noise
as the zigzag joins began to part and
the palace began to fall.

Lost in his treasure vaults, the emperor was counting the sacks, ordering them to be rearranged in a new way.

All of a sudden, he heard the clamour of masonry collapsing in the distance. 'What's that?!' he thundered.

His vizier swiped a hand through
the air and oozed reassurance.
'Surely it's nothing, Your Importantness,'
he whispered unctuously,
'but I will...'

Before he had time to finish his sentence,
the floor of the treasure vault disappeared
clean away beneath them.

The vizier, the emperor, and all the precious treasure plunged into the now choppy waters of the River Walaqa.

Spying their monarch struggling for his life,
the guards fled, the palace nothing more
than rubble around them.

With the sun touching the horizon,
the townspeople flocked to the imperial gate.

Rintin clapped his hands and addressed them. 'You are free!' he yelled. 'And never again will you be prisoners!'

He held up the rusty nail
with a bend at one end.

‘This nail is a symbol… a symbol that even the worst despot can be brought down in the simplest way. The great power is power that hangs by a thread.’

The crowd cheered.

Then a wizened old man pushed to the front.

Rintin recognized him as his neighbour, saved from the gallows in the nick of time. 'A young boy has saved us all,' the man exclaimed, 'and so I vote that we make him our king!'

There were more cheers, and Rintin was carried at shoulder height through the streets.

The emperor's launch took him across to the island, where he was reunited with his parents.

In due course Rintin was indeed made king and he ruled for many years.

He eventually married the little girl with the doll and had six sons, each one wiser and more handsome than the last.

On his desk he kept an orb
and a walnut-coloured box.

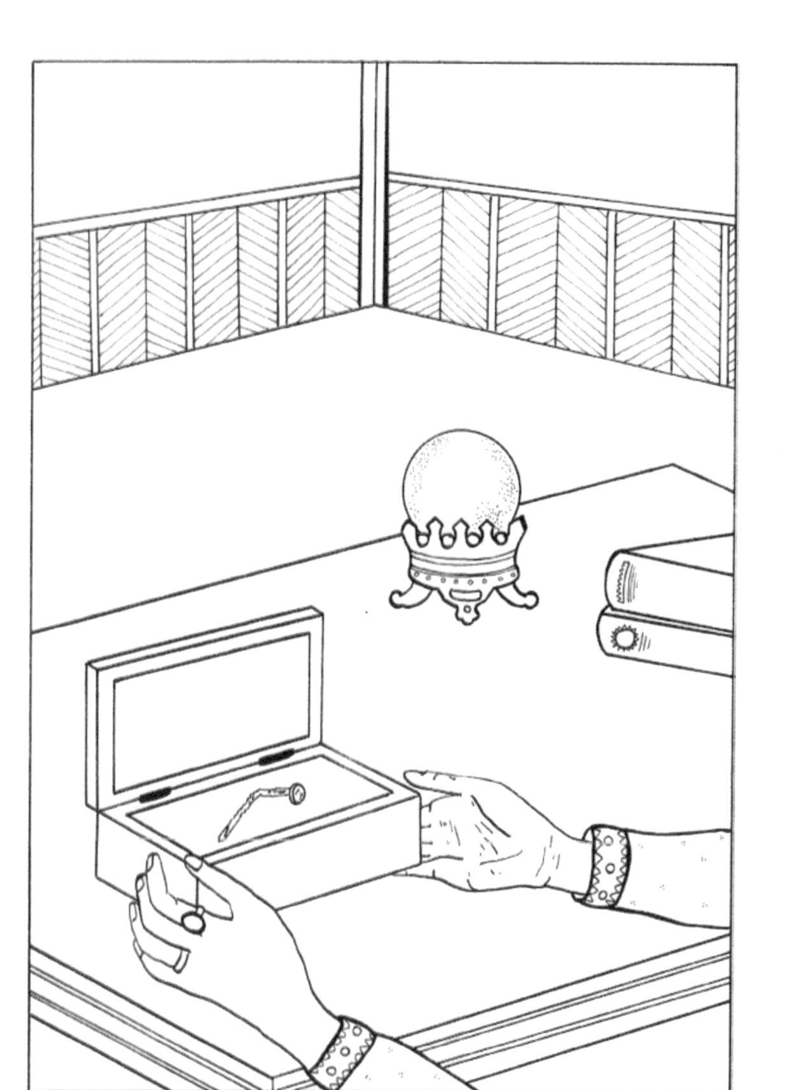

And in the box he kept the nail
– the nail that had both supported
a kingdom… and brought its end.

*Finis*

*About the Author*

Descended from a long line of storytellers, writers, and savants, Tahir Shah is one of the most prolific authors of his generation. He has published more than sixty books in numerous genres, including travel, fiction, and fantasy, as well as tales for children.

Raised in the tradition of Eastern 'teaching stories', Shah is passionate about stories and storytelling. He regards the ability to learn from folklore as being in us all, what he calls a 'default setting of humankind'. As well as having written scores of books, Shah has made documentaries for National Geographic TV and The History Channel. He is the founder and CEO of the charity, The Scheherazade Foundation.

*About the Artist*

Mahya Sadeghi was born in Iran. She studied IT and worked as a UI designer until 2016, when she decided to follow her childhood dream of becoming an artist. Mahya's passion lies in Persian miniatures, taking particular inspiration from the great Iranian painter and illustrator, Sani ol-Molk. She now works as a freelance artist on projects in Iran, Sweden, and the UK.

*Books By Tahir Shah*

*The Writer's Craft*

The Reason to Write

Workbook: Comprehensive, Volume I & II

Workbook: Fantasy, Volume I & II

Workbook: Fiction, Volume I & II

Workbook: Historical Fiction, Volume I & II

Workbook: Teaching Stories, Volume I & II

Workbook: Travel, Volume I & II

*Novels*

Jinn Hunter: Book One – The Prism

Jinn Hunter: Book Two – The Jinnslayer

Jinn Hunter: Book Three – The Perplexity

Hannibal Fogg and the Supreme Secret of Man

Casablanca Blues

Eye Spy

Godman

Paris Syndrome

Timbuctoo

Midas

Zigzagzone

*Nasrudin*

Travels With Nasrudin

The Misadventures of the Mystifying Nasrudin

The Peregrinations of the Perplexing Nasrudin

The Voyages and Vicissitudes of Nasrudin

Nasrudin in the Land of Fools

*Travel*

Trail of Feathers
Travels With Myself
Beyond the Devil's Teeth
In Search of King Solomon's Mines
House of the Tiger King
In Arabian Nights
The Caliph's House
Sorcerer's Apprentice
Journey Through Namibia

*Teaching Stories*

The Arabian Nights Adventures
Scorpion Soup
Tales Told to a Melon
The Afghan Notebook
Daydreams of an Octopus & Other Stories
The Caravanserai Stories
Ghoul Brothers
Hourglass
Imaginist
Jinn's Treasure
Jinnlore
Mellified Man
Skeleton Island
Wellspring
When the Sun Forgot to Rise
Outrunning the Reaper
The Cap of Invisibility
On Backgammon Time
The Wondrous Seed

The Paradise Tree
Mouse House
The Hoopoe's Flight
The Old Wind
A Treasury of Tales
The Tale of Double Six
The Forgotten Game
King of the Jinns
The Destiny Ring
Changing the World
Cat, Mouse
Frogland
Mittle-Mittle
Capilongo
The Princess of Zilzilam
The Singing Serpents
The Tale of the Rusty Nail
The Unicorn's Tear
The Clockmaker Who Travelled Through Time
The Fish's Dream
The Man Whose Arms Grew Branches
The Most Foolish of Men
The Shop That Sold Truth
Qwerty
Renaissance
The Man With the Tiger's Head
The Kingdom of Blink
The Wisdom of Celestine
Dream Soup
The Skeleton Factory
An Unexpected Gift

The Problem Exchange
The Pharaoh Code
The Monkey Puzzle Club
Liquid Time
Cat Dog, Dog Cat
Princess Pickle's Laugh

*Anthologies*
The Anthologies: Africa
The Anthologies: Ceremony
The Anthologies: Childhood
The Anthologies: City
The Anthologies: Danger
The Anthologies: East
The Anthologies: Expedition
The Anthologies: Frontier
The Anthologies: Hinterland
The Anthologies: India
The Anthologies: Jinns
The Anthologies: Jungle
The Anthologies: Magic
The Anthologies: Morocco
The Anthologies: Nasrudin
The Anthologies: People
The Anthologies: Quest
The Anthologies: South
The Anthologies: Taboo
The Anthologies: Teaching Stories
The Clockmaker's Box
The Tahir Shah Fiction Reader
The Tahir Shah Travel Reader

*Research*

Cultural Research

The Middle East Bedside Book

Three Essays

*Edited by*

Congress With a Crocodile

A Son of a Son, Volume I

A Son of a Son, Volume II

*Screenplays*

Casablanca Blues: The Screenplay

Timbuctoo: The Screenplay

## A REQUEST

If you enjoyed this book, please review it on your favourite online retailer or review website.

**Reviews are an author's best friend.**

To stay in touch with Tahir Shah, and to hear about his upcoming releases before anyone else, please sign up for his mailing list:

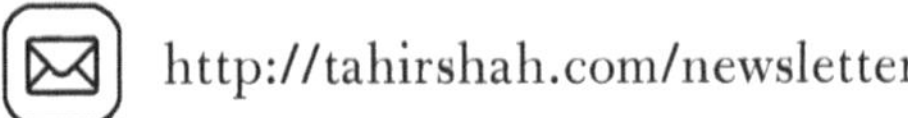

http://tahirshah.com/newsletter

And to follow him on social media, please go to any of the following links:

http://www.twitter.com/humanstew

@tahirshah999

http://www.facebook.com/TahirShahAuthor

http://www.youtube.com/user/tahirshah999

http://www.pinterest.com/tahirshah

https://www.goodreads.com/tahirshahauthor

**http://www.tahirshah.com**

www.ingramcontent.com/pod-product-compliance
Lightning Source LLC
Chambersburg PA
CBHW030523310726
48979CB00010B/1775/J
*9781915876072*